IMPOSSIBLE

Jocelyn Shipley

orca soundings

ORCA BOOK PUBLISHERS

Library and Archives Canada Cataloguing in Publication

Shipley, Jocelyn, author
Impossible / Jocelyn Shipley.
(Orca soundings)

Issued in print and electronic formats.
ISBN 978-1-4598-1556-8 (softcover).— ISBN 978-1-4598-1557-5 (PDF).—
ISBN 978-1-4598-1558-2 (EPUB)

I. Title. II. Series: Orca soundings
PS8587.H563I47 2018   jc813'.6   C2017-904497-4
                             C2017-904498-2

First published in the United States, 2018
Library of Congress Control Number: 2017949679

Summary: In this high-interest novel for teen readers,
Jemma witnesses a drive-by shooting but is afraid to speak up.

MIX
Paper from
responsible sources
FSC® C016245

*Orca Book Publishers is dedicated to preserving the environment and has
printed this book on Forest Stewardship Council® certified paper.*

Orca Book Publishers gratefully acknowledges the support for its
publishing programs provided by the following agencies: the Government
of Canada through the Canada Book Fund and the Canada Council
for the Arts, and the Province of British Columbia through
the BC Arts Council and the Book Publishing Tax Credit.

Edited by Tanya Trafford
Cover images by iStock.com and Shutterstock.com

ORCA BOOK PUBLISHERS
www.orcabook.com

Printed and bound in Canada.

21 20 19 18 • 4 3 2 1

For my readers

Chapter One

"Hey there," I say as Violet wriggles and coos on her colorful playmat. It has lots of shiny squeaky toys attached. Got it free at Swap Day in our building. "Look what Mama has for you." Violet kicks her chubby little legs and flails her arms when she sees her bottle.

I wasn't planning to be a teen mom. But now that I am, I can't imagine my life without my baby. Sometimes she's all that keeps me going.

It's a humid August night, but I lift Violet and hold her close anyway. I love the feel of her soft, smooth skin and the smell of her hair. I love how she smiles up at me, her big blue eyes full of trust.

Violet grabs at her bottle and gulps her milk down. I miss breastfeeding, but since I switched her to formula, it's way easier for Wade to babysit when I go to work. I burp her, wipe spit-up from my jean shorts and get her ready for bed.

I rock her in my arms a while before settling her into her crib beside her fluffy pink blanket and stuffed white bunny. I wind up her mobile and listen while it plays "Twinkle, Twinkle, Little Star."

Finally I turn out the light and say, "Good night, best little girl in the world." Just like my mom used to say to me. Back when she still thought I was, that is.

I push guilt from my mind and head to the fridge for a cold drink. But we're out of soda. We're also out of milk and bread for breakfast. Why the hell didn't I go to the store earlier?

I really meant to. But I'm *sooo* tired. This afternoon was so hot and muggy, I could barely move.

I fill my glass with tap water. Of course we're also out of ice cubes, because I forgot to refill the tray. I take my drink and stand by our sixth-floor window.

There's a party down in the park outside our building. People are talking and laughing, having a great time. Bringing back memories I'd rather forget.

I'd like to shut the windows to keep the sound out. But the city is stuck in a heat wave, and our air conditioner is broken. As usual.

If Wade was here, he'd help me through. He's my half brother, ten years older than me and a million years wiser. He took me in when I was pregnant and had nowhere else to go.

He's been like a father to Violet. Which is good, because her actual father doesn't know she exists. And no way will I ever tell him about her.

Because of Wade, I have a future again. He's the manager at the Bean Leaf Café, and he got me a job. Now I'm saving every penny, trying to be a good mom. When Violet is older, I'll go back to school to get my diploma.

But Wade is bartending at a friend's stag tonight, then staying over. I guess I should text him. He would probably even find somebody in the building to go to the store for me. He's on the co-op board. He knows everybody, and they all like him.

But I don't want to bother my big brother. Much as I love him, sometimes our relationship is just too parental. I'm deeply grateful for everything he's done. But I need to learn to cope by myself.

I pace the apartment, even though that makes me sweat. Our two floor fans are running full blast, but still the humidity is sickening. I feel all sticky and gross, and the air reeks of dirty diapers.

The party in the park ramps up. More people, more drinks. I step away from the window and take another look in the fridge. Wade has some beer. A cold one would taste great right now.

I open a can and chug it down. I so want another. But Wade will freak if I drink all his beer, and I can't afford to replace it.

If only it wasn't so sweltering in here. This heat's giving me brain fog. And that party in the park is making me crazy.

I pace around some more. It would be so easy to slip out for groceries. There's a 24/7 convenience store, the Ready Go, right on our corner.

Violet doesn't sleep through the night, but she never wakes up before two or three AM. I could be back in fifteen minutes max. That's no longer than I leave her alone when I go down to the laundry room.

So what's the difference if I head to the store instead?

No, no, no. Can't do that.

I am not going out and leaving my kid alone. It's illegal and dangerous. What if there's a fire?

I try to distract myself by cleaning up the kitchen.

But then the mad cravings start. I want chocolate. I want ice cream. I want cigarettes. Yeah, I know I shouldn't smoke. And I did quit when I got pregnant. But it was easy then. Smoking made me puke. Tonight I have this strong desire to light up again.

I tidy Violet's toys, fold her laundry and set out a clean onesie in case she's wet in the night. I used up the last of a package of diapers after her bath, so I look in the closet for a new one. And don't find any.

Oh shit! I mean, like, literally, right? I was sure we had lots on hand. Now I really do need to go to the store, even though diapers are ridiculously expensive at the Ready Go.

But still, I shouldn't leave Violet alone.

Maybe I could call Big Bad Betty. She's this old Korean lady down on the fourth floor. Her real name is Kim Soon-hee. Besides Wade and Dekker, the building manager's assistant, she's my only actual friend here.

Betty sometimes watches Violet for me. But nah. It's too late. Almost midnight. I'll just have to take my chances.

My shorts look okay where I wiped off the spit-up, but now I notice some on my shirt. Don't have anything else clean, so I pull on a new tank top I was saving for special, lime green with a shiny silver butterfly on the front.

I check to see that Violet's sleeping soundly before throwing my keys, phone and wallet into a cloth shopping bag.

Then I lock the door and run.

Chapter Two

I take the stairs, not the elevator, so there's less chance of being noticed. I can't risk anyone telling Wade they saw me leaving without Violet.

What a relief the cooler night air is. I glance around as I cross the street to be sure nobody's hiding in the shadows. This area is pretty safe, but I always check, even in broad daylight. Have to watch out for a certain guy I never want to see again.

It's been over a year since I escaped, and he hasn't shown up. But what if he's not the kind of guy to just let me go?

I don't see anyone lurking, so I cut across the park, keeping clear of the party. Wouldn't want to be tempted to join in. I focus on reaching the Ready Go.

Luckily, the store isn't busy. I resist the cigarettes but break down and buy a carton of chocolate-fudge ice cream along with the diapers. When the cashier checks me through, she says, "Love that top. Where'd you get it?"

"Thanks. Old Navy, final sale." I don't make eye contact, just hurry from the store. So far I haven't been gone longer than it would take to load three washing machines and put in the coins. But what if Violet wakes up? What was I thinking, leaving her alone?

Back out on the sidewalk, I spot a kid from our building, Kwame Mensah, riding his bike. Hope he doesn't see me and stop to say hey, like he does when I have Violet with me. That's all I need.

I flatten myself into the doorway of a building to hide. I'm not completely out of sight, but it works. Kwame rides right on by.

Whoa! That was close.

I step back onto the sidewalk.

And then, out of nowhere, a black SUV with its windows wide-open blasts past. I catch a glimpse of the driver as the vehicle squeals around the corner.

Just as Kwame reaches the intersection, a guy leans out the passenger window.

He's got a gun.

He fires.

Kwame and his bike go flying. The bike crashes into the curb. Kwame lands on the pavement with a sickening thud.

His crumpled body lies still.

Dead still.

Omigod, omigod, omigod!

I'm paralyzed with shock as the SUV disappears down the street. I try to scream, but no sound comes out.

I grab my phone to call 9-1-1.

But my hands are shaking so hard, I can't dial.

The driver. Those eyes. I recognized him!

Staff from the store rush out to where Kwame is lying in a pool of blood. I know I should stick around, but I break into a run. I have to get back to Violet.

Racing home, I lose one of my flip-flops. Almost without stopping, I pull off the other, toss both into my shopping bag and keep going. I make it to the building and dash up the stairs in my bare feet.

When I reach our apartment, I think I'm going to faint. Or barf. Or both.

But everything's okay. My baby is still there. She's sleeping soundly, arms holding her bunny close.

I gulp down a glass of water and collapse on my bed, soaked with sweat, trembling with fear.

Did I just witness a drive-by shooting?

Is Kwame really dead?

And was the driver really who I think it was?

But everything happened so fast. When I try to recall the details, it's all gone fuzzy.

Could I have imagined it was him?

I do tend to be paranoid. Maybe it was just somebody who looks like him. Lots of guys have big muscles from working out. Lots of guys have shaved heads and arms covered in ink.

But I saw his eyes.

Sure, it was dark out. But under the streetlight I saw his eyes.

It was Razor.

I always knew he was a criminal. But this is beyond bad. This makes him an accomplice to murder.

I want my big brother Wade to come home and look after me. I want him to make this all go away.

But I can't tell him what I saw. *Ever*. Because he'd insist I go to the police, which isn't an option. And he'd find out I left Violet home alone.

He'd be so pissed off. Drinking one of his beers was bad enough. But being irresponsible with Violet is way worse. He wouldn't care that we were out of diapers. He'd rather Violet be soaked and stinking than have me leave her. He doesn't even approve of me going down to the laundry room without her.

I can't believe I left her. How stupid was that? And I can't stop seeing

Kwame's body lying in a pool of blood in the street.

Then I'm bawling. I sob and sob and sob.

I know I should call the cops. But I'm too scared. If I admit to being a witness, I'll have to testify in court. And I could never testify against Razor.

And omigod, what if he recognized me too? Or what if the actual shooter saw me? Because if either of them did, it won't matter if I never tell a soul. They'll find me.

If only I hadn't gone out.

If only I'd never met Razor in the first place.

But I was fifteen, and nothing could keep me from a fun summer in the big city. Wade said I could stay at his place and work at the café.

When I arrived at the bus station downtown and was trying to figure out the way to the subway, this older guy asked if I needed help.

He told me his name was Ralph Stanislav but everybody called him Razor. He said he was twenty-one, but he wouldn't tell me anything else. He said it was more interesting to talk about me. That should have been a red flag, and I knew it wasn't smart to go off with a stranger.

But he was so hot. And he had such a cool car. And I'd never had a boyfriend.

I wanted adventure.

Right. I've spent the past sixteen months trying to forget Razor and everything that happened since that day at the bus station.

And now I keep seeing his ice-blue eyes as he drove by.

Such hateful, scary eyes.

Chapter Three

I wake up bathed in sweat. At first I think I had a bad dream. Then I realize I'm remembering last night. It all comes rushing back, filling me with guilt and fear.

Up until now, my biggest worry was that Razor would find out Violet is his kid. And then people would find out about my past with him. But now I've got way bigger things to obsess over. I witnessed a murder and didn't do anything.

I didn't help the victim. I didn't call the cops. I just ran home and hid.

I'm a terrible person!

But no. I did the right thing. Well, the right thing for me and Violet. I have to protect her, no matter what. It's not like I meant to witness a murder. I know I made a mistake leaving her alone, but it was just a little one.

So why are the consequences so huge?

Since I don't work today, I'd like to take Violet for a walk. We could go down to the lake to cool off. But when I look out the window to check the weather, I see cop cars and news vans everywhere.

Probably the back exit is swarmed too. Nobody's getting in or out of the building without being interviewed.

And I bet the lobby's full of people talking about the shooting.

I can't face that. No way can I be interviewed or talk to anybody. I'd break down for sure. I'd tell everything, and my life would be over.

So I'm trapped inside. I have to stay calm and not make anyone suspicious. I have to look after Violet.

As if she knows what I'm thinking, she wakes up. Smiles and reaches her little arms out to me. Makes these *mmmmm* sounds that could be words, not just baby talk. I'm pretty sure she's trying to say "mama." I concentrate on that rather than on how much her eyes look like her father's.

And how in love with his eyes I once was.

When Violet's bottle is ready, I turn on the TV. The shooting is all over the news. I hate watching, but I can't not watch. I have to know what they're saying.

First there's an interview with the cashier from Ready Go. She says there was a young woman in the store just before it happened. *Holy shit!* But all she remembers is my lime-green tank top with the butterfly, and that I bought diapers. Then she shakes her head and starts to cry, hiding her face in her hands.

Lucky for me, the security cameras weren't working. I never even thought about video evidence. But there is none, so I can't be identified that way.

The reporter says that homicide detectives are asking the young woman who was shopping in Ready Go just before the shooting to contact them. *Omigod!* Never! And I'm pitching that tank top.

They're also asking anyone who witnessed the brutal murder of a thirteen-year-old boy to come forward. Anyone with any information at all.

Then there's an interview with Kwame's father. Mr. Mensah is devastated but dignified. He speaks of Kwame with so much love. He begs for someone to explain what happened. He and his family need to know who did it and why.

I start to sob again. I remember Kwame finding a rattle for Violet at Swap Day. And I've met his mom, Amadi, at co-op meetings. She's lovely. I can't imagine what she's going through right now.

I hold Violet so tight, she squirms and whimpers.

I set her down on her playmat. I feel sick. I know what happened, but I just can't tell Kwame's parents. I'm too terrified of Razor.

My phone rings, and I panic. But it's not him. It's Wade.

"You see the news?" he says. "That kid from our building who got shot?"

"Yeah, I have it on right now." Violet tries to crawl off her playmat. She'll be mobile soon and getting into everything. We've already made the apartment child friendly, but she's going to be so much harder to watch. How am I ever going to keep her safe? "It's horrible," I say. "Kwame was such a sweet kid."

"I know," Wade says. "I know. I already left a message for his family. And the co-op board wants to start a fund for them, to help with funeral expenses and so on."

"Good idea." Trust Wade to be thinking of the family while all I did was sit here worrying about my own sorry ass.

"And Jem? I was wondering if you could maybe look after organizing that?"

"What? Me?" *Can't. Can't. Can't.*

"Well, I know you knew them, and I thought you'd want to help."

"Of course I want to help," I say. "But I only knew them a little bit. Like, not well or anything."

"It would be a good way for you to contribute to the Woodley Co-op."

Wade's right. Everybody who lives here is supposed to volunteer in some way. Since Violet was born, I haven't been doing my part. If I don't agree, he'll wonder why. "Well, okay, I guess. But you'll have to tell me how. I mean, do I go door to door or what?"

"Thanks, Jem. We can figure out the logistics tonight. You could start by putting a sign up on the bulletin board, and maybe post something on the website. Violet okay?"

"She's good."

"You okay?"

No, I'm not. I'm scared shitless. And I just agreed to collect money for Kwame's family, which means talking to everybody in the building. "Fine. You'll be home for dinner?"

"Not until after ten. Some of the guys are going to the ball game."

"Okay, have fun." I don't want Wade to know how I'm really feeling. He'd be home and have the truth out of me in minutes. He'd force me to go to the cops.

My brother always does the right thing. That's why he's such a good co-op board member. I mean, he already thought to set up a fund. He already called Kwame's family. I'm sure he left the nicest message, full of sympathy and support.

And here I am, keeping what I saw a secret.

The Mensahs have a right to know who murdered their son. I really wish I could help them out.

But I can't face what will happen if I tell.

Chapter Four

I spend the afternoon playing with Violet and thinking things through. I need to keep my story straight, especially around Wade. And my story is that I don't know anything.

If by chance that cashier remembers more details, or somehow somebody figures out it was me in Ready Go, I'll admit to being there. I'll admit to leaving

Violet alone to buy diapers. I'll take the consequences, whatever they are.

But I'll swear I didn't see anything. I'll say I heard the shot but was already halfway home. I was scared by the sound and ran back to my baby. I didn't call the cops because I didn't witness the shooting. So I don't have anything to tell them.

I wrap my lime-green tank top in plastic bags and stuff it down the garbage chute. Now I just have to figure out how to help with the memorial fund.

It's going to be brutal. How can I keep from sobbing when I ask people in our building to contribute? As soon as I say how nice the Mensahs are, and how shocked and horrified I am that something like this could happen, I'll burst into tears. I'll have to hope that if I cry, people will think it's because Kwame was my friend. Not because I witnessed his murder.

Collecting for the fund might actually be a good thing though. It will make me look innocent. Everyone will think I'm great for helping out.

Yeah, I know that sounds selfish and heartless. And it totally is. But as much as I want to help the Mensahs, I can't tell them anything. That would be way too dangerous.

I'm super worried about putting a sign on the bulletin board like Wade suggested. If I see Big Bad Betty or Dekker in the mail room, I'll crack for sure.

But I have to do something.

And then I have a brilliant idea. What if I tell people to leave their donations at the building manager's office? The money would be safer there than here in our apartment. And I wouldn't have to go door to door.

I log in to Wade's laptop and email Dekker to ask him to check if that would be okay. Since we're friends, he responds right away, saying what a good plan it is. He asks if I'm coming by the office soon. I sometimes bring Violet down for a visit.

I really want to see him. He's such a nice guy. Not that I'm looking for romance. But if I ever was, I'd have my eye on him. Okay, I kind of already do.

But my best bet is to act normal and avoid talking to anybody. So I tell Dekker that maybe I'll visit, and then I post a notice about the memorial fund on the members' section of Woodley Co-op's website.

After dinner Violet plays happily on her mat. I try to watch a movie to distract myself. But nothing takes my mind off my problems.

How I wish Wade would come home. When he's going to be late, he always calls to check that we're okay. So when my phone rings I'm sure it's him, and I don't even glance at the caller ID.

"Hey, how's it going?" I say. "Things are good here." I try to sound in control, so Wade won't pick up on my fear.

"Hey, babe," a steely voice says.

I freeze. I'd know that voice anywhere.

"How did you get this number?" I ditched my phone when I left Razor. Wade bought me a new one when Violet was born, since we don't have a landline.

"Babe," Razor says. "I can get anything."

Of course he can. He's Razor. He never came after me, but that doesn't mean he couldn't find me. He just never needed to. Until now.

"What do you want?" As if I don't know. I should hang up and turn my phone off. But it wouldn't help.

"Did you really think you could just walk out on me?"

Actually, I did. I know that sounds stupid. But he always had other girls on the side. I even thought he might have been glad to be rid of me. We'd been fighting over the things he wanted me to do. I figured he'd go back to the bus station and find a new me in minutes.

"Please leave me alone."

"Now why would I want to do that?"

"Because it's over. There's nothing more to say."

"You sure? 'Cause I think we got something to discuss."

So he *did* recognize me when he drove by. *Shit*. Did he tell the shooter?

If he did, I'm dead.

I can't speak. I just stand there, shaking.

Violet chooses that moment to let out a long, hungry wail. It's time for her last bottle. I set down my phone, pull her into my arms and stick a soother in her mouth.

When I pick up my phone again, I hear Razor laughing. "That a baby crying?"

"What? A baby? God no."

"Yeah, it is. You got a kid?"

"Me? Are you joking? No way. Must be from across the hall." He can't find out about Violet. I don't want him anywhere near her. "There's always some kid crying in this building."

"Right," Razor says. "So anyway, you didn't answer my question yet."

"What question?"

"Did you really think you could just walk out on me?"

I still don't answer him. Finally he says, "Oh, Jem." He laughs again, and this time it's more of a nasty snarl. "I can't let you go for good."

"Please, please, please." I remember how he liked me to beg for things. "Just leave me alone, and I won't say anything."

"About what?"

"You know what." I'm not going to mention the shooting out loud. "I promise."

"Oh, but see..." He pauses, and it sounds like he's puffing on a cigarette. It makes me want one so bad I could scream. "See, I'm not sure I can trust you."

"Of course you can." I'd like to remind him of all the times I did what he said. Times I'm ashamed of now. "Honest, you can trust me. Totally."

"But you ran out on me."

"I'm sorry I left without saying goodbye." And in a weird way, I am. In spite of all the bad stuff, we did have some good times. That's the reason I stayed as long as I did. "Please," I beg again. "I promise I'll never say anything to anybody."

"Yeah, but here's the problem," Razor says. "I just don't believe you."

Chapter Five

"You look beat," Wade says as he buckles Violet into her high chair at breakfast.

"I had a bad night," I say. I'm mixing up some rice cereal in Violet's special duck dish. "Couldn't stop thinking about that shooting. I just feel so bad for Kwame's family, you know?"

"Yeah, for sure." Wade ties a bib on Violet and starts feeding her. "But at least we're collecting for them. I saw the notice on the website. That was a good idea, to have the money dropped off."

"Sorry I didn't get anything on the bulletin board yet." Word will get around, but I still should put up an official notice. "I'll do it this morning. Any details on the funeral?"

"As soon as the police release the body. Which should be today, so they'll probably bury Kwame tomorrow."

"We'll be going, right?"

"No, it's private. Just for family. But there'll be a memorial here in the common room on Wednesday afternoon."

I stop pouring a glass of juice. "But you work then."

"I'll have to see who can cover for me."

"You have to find somebody." I don't want to go to the memorial without Wade. "Please find somebody." My voice sounds all watery, and I fight back tears.

"You okay?"

I shrug and sniffle. "Fine. Just feeling a little emotional about everything."

"Understandable. You good to work tonight?"

"Yeah, sure." I can't let Wade know anything's wrong. He's given me everything I need to turn my life around. He buys the groceries and pays the rent. While we're on the wait list for a two-bedroom, he sleeps on the futon so Violet and I can have the bedroom.

But in return, he expects me to grow up. He expects me to be mature and responsible.

When I met Razor, I was the stereotypical love-sick teenager. I believed everything he said. And he knew all the buttons to push.

You're so pretty, he said. *With some makeup and the right clothes, you could look really glamorous. You could be my girl.*

But he wanted me ready and willing to party whenever he called, so I let Wade down a ton of times. I messed up on my co-op jobs, like helping with grounds cleanup and delivering the newsletter, and I missed shifts at the Bean Leaf.

Wade wanted me to break it off. My mom wanted me to come home. Both could see what I couldn't—that Razor was trouble. But of course I wouldn't listen, so finally Wade kicked me out.

No big deal, right? I just moved in with Razor. And that's when things stopped being so much fun.

Suddenly Razor thought he owned me. He didn't want me to make any friends. He didn't want me to work. He didn't want me to go out at all.

And then he started making me do things I wasn't comfortable with. Sex stuff.

Hearing Razor's voice again on the phone last night brought it all back. No wonder I couldn't sleep.

God, I was so naïve.

Wade gives Violet a quick kiss on the top of her head. "Later," he says. He's opening the café today, so he has to be there early. As he leaves he adds, "Be a good girl, sweetheart."

I'm not sure which one of us he means. But I know he'll think about kicking me out and going for custody of Violet if he finds out what I did.

I finish feeding Violet and wipe off her face and hands. Put her down on her mat to play. Then I take a piece of printer paper and make a sign about raising funds for the Mensahs. I use every colored marker we have. I want it to look upbeat and positive, so people will donate lots of money.

When I've finished, I look out the window and notice the news vans have disappeared. Maybe they've already caught Razor and the shooter?

I check the news on TV. No such luck. They're still begging for information. But a protest over a new development on the waterfront has turned ugly, and there was a stabbing on the subway, so now those are the top stories.

I change Violet and pop her in the stroller. Grit my teeth and get on the elevator. At least there's no one around. It's Monday morning, and most people are at work or still asleep. I post the sign

I made on the bulletin board and head outside.

It rained in the night, and the morning is crisp and cool. So refreshing after all the heat. I'm a bit worried that Razor will come looking for me, so I do my usual check around the area. But I don't see him. I feel almost okay as I push Violet to the park down the block.

The park has a playground and wading pool, so there are always lots of people there with their kids. But I don't know any of them.

For the first six months after I left Razor, I was trying to heal emotionally and cope with being pregnant. Then Violet was born. The next seven months were pretty fuzzy too, what with looking after a new baby and working at the café.

I had no time or energy to socialize. Plus, I didn't want anybody asking about my past. So all these regulars at the park are strangers to me.

I take another good look around before entering. Besides the usual parents and kids, there are two life-guards at the wading pool, a crew of gardeners and some guys doing road repairs in the intersection. No Razor.

Violet is asleep in the stroller now, so I plunk down on a bench in the shade. I just want to sit here and think of nothing.

But somebody sits down beside me right away. Somebody with a big, scary dog. I don't look at him, but I get a creepy feeling. There must be five other benches. Why'd he have to pick this one?

And then I know. He picked this bench because I'm sitting here. And he wants to scare me.

It's Razor.

Chapter Six

Razor must have been hiding in a parked car or something. He's sneaky that way.

I turn and glare at him.

I have to admit, he looks good. That rugged face, those broad shoulders, those ice-blue eyes. That's why it was so hard to leave, no matter how bad he treated me. I was pathetically attracted to him. But no more.

"So," he says. "You *do* have a kid."

I kick the brake off Violet's stroller. With all these people around, he probably won't try to abduct us or anything. But still. I might need to run.

"No, I don't. She's not mine. I'm just babysitting."

"Right."

I point at his ugly dog. "New?" Razor never kept any pets. Not animal ones anyway.

Razor ignores my question and stares at my boobs. Why did I wear such a skimpy T-shirt? "Christ, Jem," he says, "you're still so hot!"

"Stop," I say. "Please."

"You've lost too much weight though." He goes to pat my arm, but I slap him away.

"Don't touch me!"

Violet shifts and stretches in her sleep. Thank God I pulled her wide-brimmed sun hat down over her eyes.

42

Razor tilts his head and studies her. "Hey there, cutie pie." He reaches out to take her hand.

I throw myself between him and Violet. "Don't touch her either!"

His dog growls and leaps at me, way too close to Violet. I move to shield her.

He yanks the leash, choking the dog back. "It's okay, Ace. They're not dangerous." Razor smirks at me. "Relax, Jem. I wouldn't hurt your little baby girl."

My insides turn to jelly. "I told you, she's not mine." There's a shrill of fear in my voice. "I just babysit her." I breathe deeply, trying to stay calm.

"You know, babe," Razor says, "I could always tell when you're lying." He strokes my hand instead of Violet's. I remember how his touch used to set me on fire.

I have to think clearly. What would Wade tell me to do? Act tough. Stand up to him. Run the fuck away.

Razor lifts his hand to my hair. I didn't tie it back today, so it's all loose and curly. He strokes it softly, just like he used to.

Nobody's touched me in a long time. Except for Violet. And a baby pulling on your hair just isn't the same.

But I know how fast Razor's touch can change. I want to scream at him to keep his hands off me. Somehow I manage to stay perfectly still.

Ace bares his teeth and growls. Strains against the leash, bashing into the stroller.

Which, of course, wakes Violet up. She whimpers a bit, then settles again.

"Hey, hey, that's good—stay asleep." I rock her back and forth in the stroller, but it doesn't work.

She wakes up, and her little arms reach to take off her sun hat. She hates wearing it. I try to stop her. "Leave your hat on, honey. It's so pretty." And it *is* pretty. Multicolored polka dots with a white ribbon bow. I hold the hat down on her.

But Violet wriggles her head away. She pulls the hat off completely and flings it to the ground. Then she smiles up at Razor.

"Fucking hell!" he says. "She's mine!"

"She's not!"

"Yeah, she is. Got my freakin' eyes." He pauses and then turns and says coldly, "And you never even told me."

Ace growls and leaps around like crazy. I'm afraid Razor's going to lose control of his dog. Or himself.

I don't know what to say next. I so don't want to get into this with him.

"Hey, I got a right to know." Razor grabs my shoulders and shakes me. "Got a right to my own kid. There's laws."

"Laws?" I say, trembling all over. "Since when did you care about laws?"

"Since it suits me." He lets go of me, and his voice softens. "Since I want to spend time with my kid, get to know her."

"Right. Like you're a real family man."

"I been thinking about it lately. My new girl's crazy to have a kid."

"So why don't you go have one with her and leave us alone."

"Not happening." Razor stares at Violet. "Wow. Can't believe I've got a kid. What's her name?"

"Not telling you."

More growling and jumping from Ace. Razor yanks on the leash and smacks him hard on the head.

The dog cowers.

I feel sorry for him. I'm familiar with Razor's fists. Been there, done that. And I'm never, ever going back. How could I possibly have found him attractive just a few minutes ago?

"C'mon, I'm the baby daddy," Razor says. "What's her name?"

"Fuck off and leave us alone!"

"And if I don't?"

"Then I'm going to the cops."

"Bad idea."

"You helped shoot an innocent kid! You belong in prison."

"Hey, I owed a guy, so I had to drive. But that's all I did. Drive. Never thought he was gonna shoot that kid. Said he just wanted to talk to him, give him a warning."

"You're still guilty."

"Well, guess what? That kid wasn't exactly innocent."

"Not what his family says."

"The family never knows the truth."

"Still doesn't make it okay. And what did he do that was so bad he had to die?"

Razor yawns and stretches. "Nothing, really. It was just a message. To somebody we can't afford to shoot."

"That's disgusting! *You're* disgusting!"

"But you still love me anyway, don't you, babe?"

"You wish." I stand and grab the stroller. Time to get the hell out of here. I don't want Violet around Razor a second longer.

"Wanna know how we got that loser dealing drugs for us?" Razor says to my back. "By watching your building. I been keeping an eye out all along. Never saw you with my baby girl, or I would have paid you a visit sooner. But that kid was a bonus. Teen from a strict family, wanting easy money. Wasn't hard to reel him in."

I grip the stroller handles hard and start walking away from Razor as fast as I can. But I still hear him call out, "See ya around, Jem."

Chapter Seven

I run all the way back to Woodley Co-op. Violet has a bumpy ride in her stroller, but I don't care. We have to get home fast.

Razor doesn't follow. But then, that's not his style. He'll probably show up somewhere else when I'm not expecting it.

The camera crews are camped out in front of our building again, so I sneak around back. But to reach the elevator, I have to go through the lobby. There's a bunch of residents gathered, Big Bad Betty among them. They're all hugging each other and crying.

While I was out, they made a display about Kwame's life. There's an easel with pictures from his birth right up to this year's school photo. There's a table with his drumsticks, soccer ball and uniform all laid out.

I want to sneak upstairs and hide like I did yesterday. But it's too late. They see me and all start talking at once, about the shooting, the fund and the memorial service.

I feel like a pile of crap. That poor, sweet kid. I don't care what Razor got him into—Kwame wasn't a criminal. He didn't deserve to be shot. His family didn't deserve to lose him.

Big Bad Betty grabs Violet out of her stroller. "Pretty flower," she says, hugging Violet to her chest. "Keep safe. Always safe."

I burst into tears. Even though she's seventy-three, Betty's the closest thing I have to a girlfriend these days. She hands Violet to someone else and flings her arms around me. Luckily, Violet doesn't make strange yet. She smiles and coos at whoever is holding her.

I'm a head taller than Betty, so it's more like she's hugging my stomach. Her face is pushed into my boobs. I'm looking down into the white roots of her dyed-black hair.

"Is okay," she says. "All gonna be okay."

But it's not. That's the problem. This isn't a dream. I'm not going to wake up and find out that the shooting never happened. I'm not going to open my eyes and remember that I didn't really witness a murder. A cold-blooded murder involving my ex, who is also the father of my baby.

No, this is for real. And I'm guilty of keeping what I saw secret.

I'm not sure if I'm crying for Kwame, his family or myself. Probably all three. At least nobody seems surprised. After all, everybody else is weeping too.

I break away from Betty. "Sorry," I say. "I have to go. I'll come and see you soon." I grab my baby back and hold her tight. "She's hungry," I tell the group. "Time for her bottle."

I rush to the elevator and push the button.

After I feed Violet, I make myself a sandwich and a cup of tea. I check the TV again to see what they're saying about the shooting. But there's nothing new.

There have been no arrests. There aren't even any leads. The investigation is "ongoing."

Violet turns herself over and over on her mat. She's figured out that she can move around by rolling. Then she reaches for the rattle that Kwame gave her. Sticks it in her mouth and gums it. Shaped like a flower, with a mirror on one side and a happy face on the other, it's pretty much her favorite toy.

I love that she likes it so much. But at the moment I can't bear to watch her play with it. "Okay, best little girl in the world," I say, gently taking the rattle out of her tight grasp and picking her up. "Time for your nap." She snuggles into my arms, and I smother her with kisses.

When Violet's asleep, I lie down on the sofa. I have to work tonight, and I've had almost no sleep since I witnessed the shooting. I pass out right away and almost can't wake up when Violet starts to fuss about two hours later.

I check my phone and see that Dekker has texted, asking if we're coming down for a visit. I'm so tempted. I've got some time to fill before dinner, and I need to keep busy. Plus, we usually go see him when the building manager is on her break, so it might seem weird if we don't.

I fix my hair, put on some makeup and carry Violet down to the office.

"Hey, Dek," I say when I enter. "Wasn't that terrible about the shooting?" His casual white shirt looks great with his dark hair and eyes.

"Tragic." He rests his elbows on the desk and his head in his hands. "Just totally tragic."

"How's the family holding up?"

"They're devastated. But they're strong, you know, and religious. So that helps."

"I guess." I shift Violet to my other hip. She's getting too heavy to carry around. "But I can't imagine how anybody ever deals with something like that."

Dekker lifts his head and grimaces. "And the worst thing is, they still don't know who did it. They don't even have any suspects."

"That really sucks." Violet pulls at my hair with her tiny fingers, making me cringe at the memory of Razor stroking my hair in the park this morning. "How's the memorial fund going?"

Dekker's face brightens. "Great. Thanks for setting that up. People have been really generous. We've got over a thousand bucks so far."

"Seriously? That's amazing! So is there anything else I need to do?"

"Not really. We'll deposit everything and cut the family one big check."

"Okay." Good news for me. But it also means I haven't done enough to count for my volunteer hours.

I can't believe I just thought that. I should be thinking about helping the Mensah family.

Dekker tickles Violet under her chin. "Hey there, gorgeous." She gives him her adorable baby giggle.

I say, "So I'll see you at the memorial service?"

"Of course." Our eyes meet. He looks a bit awkward and then blurts out, "Maybe this isn't the right time, but I've been meaning to ask. You ever want to go for coffee?"

Yes! Totally. I try to sound casual. "Sure. Just not at the Bean Leaf, okay?"

"Okay."

"Which reminds me. I'm working tonight, so I better go."

I feel even guiltier when I get back upstairs. I'm excited about our possible date but relieved Dekker didn't guess my terrible secret. He wasn't suspicious at all.

What will he think of me if he ever finds out?

Chapter Eight

"Just go, Jem," Wade says. "I'll clean up the kitchen and give Violet her bath."

"I know, I know." I have to go to work, but I'm still shaken from seeing Razor in the park this morning. I keep fiddling around with last-minute stuff. Like putting on more makeup and then wiping most of it off. Like doing my hair for the third time. "Have you seen my keys? And my phone?"

"They're in your bag," Wade says. "You put them there a minute ago."

"Oh yeah, right. I forgot." God, I'm a mess. I'm so jittery that at dinner I spilled tomato sauce all down my Bean Leaf T-shirt and black skirt. Since my extra uniform is in the laundry basket, I had to sponge the mess off. Now there's a big wet patch from my chest right down to my crotch.

I am dreading going to work. And not just because of Razor. I don't want to have to walk past the site of the shooting. But there isn't time to go another way.

Wade hands me my bag and pushes me toward the door. He holds Violet up for me to kiss goodbye. "Now boot it. You're gonna be late. And your manager hates that."

"Sorry." Wade is such a good boss. And I'd say that even if he wasn't my big brother. All the staff like and respect him. "Sorry, sorry, sorry." If he only knew what I'm really sorry for.

Wade's a great babysitter too. I never worry about Violet when she's with him. By the time I get home at eleven, she'll have had her last bottle. She'll be in her crib, sound asleep.

I head up the street, walking fast. Staring straight ahead. But my mind replays it all.

The black SUV roars up again. As it squeals around the corner, I see Razor driving. The other guy leans out the window and shoots.

Kwame is lifted up off his bike and into the air.

Now there's a shrine near where Kwame landed.

The sidewalk in front of Ready Go is piled with flowers and candles and photos and toys. The display in the building lobby was sad, but this is heartbreaking.

Some of it must be from Kwame's friends. But a lot is from the general public. People who didn't even know him but still want to honor him.

I wonder about adding something to the remembrances. But what? There's already so much stuff here.

Maybe I could bring the rattle he gave Violet? But I'd rather she kept that. Wouldn't it be a better way to remember Kwame? By seeing how much she likes it every day?

A girl about Kwame's age comes by and adds a mixed bouquet to the pile. Tears stream down her face. "Did you know him?" she asks me.

"Yeah, kind of. He lived in the same building as me. What about you?"

"He was my best friend," she sobs. "And my first boyfriend."

"Sorry," I say. "Oh God, I'm so, so sorry."

I walk on to give her some privacy. Grief floods over me. For her, for the life Kwame will never have and for the Mensah family.

Knowing who did it would at least give Kwame's parents some closure. I'm sure they'd welcome that. For their sakes, I wish I could go to the cops.

But I can't. I have to do what's best for Violet.

I walk on to work, hating myself. I made a bad decision leaving Violet alone and going to the store that night. I know the shooting would have happened anyway. But now I'm paying the price of being a witness. And the debt is one I can never clear.

Is it true that Razor didn't know Kwame would be shot? Should I believe him? And does it even matter? He's still guilty of being an accomplice. He's still evil.

What matters more is, did the shooter see me? And if he did, will Razor protect my identity? Or will he tell him who I am?

It's Monday night, so not much is happening in the neighborhood. The Bean Leaf isn't busy at all. I could sit and read a magazine. But I'm too jumpy. So I clean tables and refill the milk, cream and sugars.

I watch the door the whole the time, just in case. Razor was toying with me in the park today. He wants to keep me off-balance.

Well, he succeeded.

I'm rattled.

And I can't stop remembering things I'd rather forget.

How I wish I'd listened to Wade and my mom. How I wish I'd asked more questions about Razor's work, which turned out to be drug and porn related, before I moved in with him. Or that I'd at least demanded answers to the ones I did ask.

But he made tons of money. He bought me cool clothes and expensive jewelry. He took me to fancy bars and restaurants and fantastic parties.

He rented a nice, respectable detached family home in the eastern suburbs. Landscaped front yard. All very well kept. What more did I need to know?

So when Wade kicked me out, it seemed like a good idea to forget my family and go live with Razor.

But after Razor had made me completely dependent on him, he said I had to earn my keep. With his friends. While he recorded everything.

I can't believe now that I ever went along with it.

He didn't lock me in or anything. Didn't have to. I was totally stuck in my own mess. No job. No friends. No self-respect. Whenever I did threaten to leave, Razor would remind me of his photo and video collection. Did I want my mother and brother to see that?

"Hello? Can we get some service here, please?"

A hipster couple has come into the café. I take their order, still in a daze.

"Hey," the guy says. "I wanted an Americano, not a large black decaf."

The woman says, "And I ordered iced black currant tea, not a chai latte."

"Sorry." I dump their drinks and start again. I get them right this time, but then I mess up the change.

I'm so upset by the time I've closed the café that I take a taxi home. I can't really afford such a luxury. But I'm too scared to walk. Because I know it's only a matter of time before Razor makes his next move.

Chapter Nine

In the morning I can hardly drag myself out of bed. I didn't fall asleep until long after midnight. Now it's six thirty, and Violet's crying. I lean over her crib and try to shush her, but she won't settle back down. She's hungry.

I lift her and tiptoe past the futon in the living room. Don't want to wake Wade.

I shut the kitchen door and get a bottle ready.

When Violet's had her milk, I sit her in her high chair. Pour some Cheerios on the tray. She loves to pick them up and stuff them in her mouth or hurl them onto the floor. Keeps her busy.

I make strong coffee. Open the box of day-old baking I brought home from the café last night. There are blueberry muffins, cheese scones and oatmeal cookies. Normally, I'd want one of each. But today I can't face eating.

I'm too exhausted. Too guilty. Too scared.

After Wade leaves for work, I vacuum the apartment, clean the bathroom and even scrub the kitchen sink. Anything to keep my mind off Razor.

But I can't block him out. The thought of what he might do is terrifying.

And what about the actual shooter? If he does know I am a witness, he's not going to just let me be. He's going to make sure I don't rat.

The pressure is too much. I have to talk to someone or I'll freak.

But there's only Betty. I've been avoiding a visit because I'm afraid she'll get the truth out of me. They don't call her Big Bad Betty for nothing. For such a tiny person, she can be very intimidating. She's on the co-op board, and everybody's scared of her. Except for Wade. They adore each other.

But I really need some company right now. So I take Violet and some muffins down to the fourth floor. Betty answers her door like she was waiting for us. Which she probably was. We often stop by around this time of day.

"Come, come," she says, pulling us in. "See what I make."

Betty creates cool jewelry with fine silken cords of all colors. She ties them into fancy knots. Apparently, it's an ancient Korean craft. "For Amadi," she says, holding up a necklace. The knots look like beads. Betty has used shades of red, orange and gold.

"Oh, wow, that's beautiful."

Betty nods. "To remember her boy Kwame." She reaches out to take Violet. "Happy flower face," she says. "So precious."

"Brought you some muffins." I hand her the bag.

"Thanks," Betty says. "Tea?"

"Tea would be great." I take Violet back and sit on Betty's floral sofa. It almost matches the flowered stretch pants she's wearing today. Violet loves the sofa's pattern and colors. She grabs at the cushions like she wants to pick the flowers.

Betty puts the muffins on a plate and sets it on the coffee table. She makes jasmine tea in a black iron pot and pours me a cup. Violet grabs for that too.

"No, no, sweetie. Too hot." I break off a piece of muffin for her. She jams it into her mouth, and crumbs fall everywhere. She struggles in my arms, trying to get more.

Betty takes Violet again and gives her another piece of muffin. Then she scrunches up her face and peers at me. "Nobody come forward about Kwame," she says. "Nobody will tell what happen."

"I know," I say. "It's so sad."

"That woman," Betty says. "On TV."

"The cashier?"

"No, the one wearing tank top. Buying diapers." Betty hands Violet back and picks up some bright-blue cords. She starts knotting them like she's strangling someone. "She should tell."

"Maybe she didn't see anything." Good thing I stuffed that tank top down the garbage chute. And thank heavens

I only wore it that night, and neither Betty nor Wade saw me.

Betty nods and says, "Must have seen something." She concentrates on the cords. "She should tell." Her fingers move fast and furious. The intricate knot starts to look like a dragonfly.

Violet leans forward, trying to get hold of it. "What if she can't tell anybody?" I say.

Betty scowls. "Why not?"

"Dunno. Maybe she's scared? Maybe she doesn't want to have to testify in court?"

"What about Amadi?" Betty pulls the cords out of Violet's reach. "Her boy dead."

At the mention of Amadi's loss, something inside me breaks. "Yeah, you're right." I should go to the police station right now. It's only four blocks away.

But no. I just can't. Wade will find out I left Violet home alone that night. He'll never forgive me. And Razor will kill me!

"Crime Stoppers," Betty says.

"You think she should call them?"

"They don't say your name. Mr. Mensah told me."

"He did?"

"He say nobody find out. Safe, safe."

"I guess," I say.

"Could be reward," Betty says. "Lots of money."

Interesting. Could they possibly pay me enough to turn Razor in? "What if it's still too big a risk?"

Betty shrugs and pours more tea. We drink it in silence. There's really nothing else to talk about. But even if Big Bad Betty suspects it was me in Ready Go, she doesn't know for sure.

I head back upstairs to the apartment and feed Violet again. I put her down for her nap. I lie on my bed and try to sleep too. But of course I can't.

What to do? What to do? What to do?

Chapter Ten

"You okay?" Wade says at dinner. "You look worried."

I concentrate on cutting up the roast chicken he bought at the deli. He also got potato salad, coleslaw and crusty bread. My favorite meal. "Yeah, sure. I'm fine." He holds out his plate, and I fill it for him. "I mean, I'm still upset about the shooting, but that's normal, right?"

"Of course." Wade tries to make eye contact. I pretend to be busy serving myself some chicken. But when I sit down at the table, he's still looking at me. "Anything else?"

"I guess I'm just really tired," I say. "I haven't been sleeping much."

"Why's that?"

"Oh, you know. Violet fusses in the middle of the night, and then it's been so hot and all." Violet drops her spoon, and I pick it up for her. "Hey, were you able to get somebody to cover for you tomorrow?"

"Sorry, no." Wade starts eating his dinner. "Everybody's either sick or on holidays."

"But it's Kwame's memorial!" I don't want to go without Wade.

"Jem," Wade says. "Do you think I didn't try? I'm on the co-op board, for Christ's sake. Of course I'd go if I could."

I almost offer to work for him. Anything to get out of facing the Mensah family. But that would make Wade suspicious. "Yeah, I know. Sorry." I get a cloth to wipe Violet's face and hands. "But can't you just put a Closed sign on the door?"

"No."

"That's so not fair."

"Well, that's what being manager means. It all comes down to me."

"Still," I say. "I wish you could come."

Wade gives me this look. I know it so well. When I was a little kid, he always knew when I was hiding something. He still does.

When I escaped from Razor and came here pregnant and desperate, it didn't take Wade long to find out everything. He wanted me to press charges. But I just wanted to forget. So I said no. Now, though, I kind of wish I had. Because Razor would be in jail, and maybe Kwame would still be alive.

I'm tempted to tell Wade about the shooting. The relief would be so great. And no matter how pissed off he'd be, I think he'd help me.

But just as I'm about to cave, Wade gets up. "Okay," he says, clearing his plate. "I'm off to hit some home runs."

He plays in a slow-pitch league. I'd forgotten he has a game tonight. Now I've missed my chance to confess.

Or maybe I'm just too scared. He'd stay home if I told him what happened.

I lift Violet from her high chair and cuddle her. "Who's my sweet flower?" I say. "Who's the best little girl in the world?" She pulls on my hair and laughs.

I hold her even closer. How would I cope if anything ever happened to her?

After dinner I clean up the kitchen. Then I try to watch TV. But, just like the other night, nothing distracts me.

All I want to do is check the news. They're still talking about the shooting. Still asking the young woman who was in Ready Go to call. Still begging witnesses to come forward. Still playing Mr. Mensah's plea for information from the public.

Nothing's changed, which I guess is good for me. But not for Kwame's family. I feel so terrible not telling them what I know. But I'd feel worse if I did.

I don't know what to do for the rest of the evening. I'd like to take Violet for a walk, since we've been in all day. But I'm scared to go outdoors in case Razor shows up again.

So how to fill the time? Sit here and obsess about what's going to happen? Worry about facing the Mensahs at the memorial tomorrow? Fight off fear of what Razor might be planning?

I'm almost glad when there's a knock at the door. Probably Betty, come to see how I'm doing. I think about not answering, but I know she won't go away. So I open the door.

It's not Betty.

It's Razor.

Chapter Eleven

Razor's wearing jeans that fit perfectly and a T-shirt that shows off his tats. He looks like a movie star. But not the hero. The bad guy.

"Hey, babe," he says with a grin. "Knew you'd be happy to see me."

"No, I'm not." I try to push the door shut. "Go away, or I'll call the cops."

"Seriously?" He forces the door open with one hand. With the other, he twists my arm up behind my back. "I can't let you do that, Jem."

I struggle, but I'm helpless against him. "Let me go!"

Razor grips my arm tighter. Hurts like hell.

He forces me into the living room, pushes me onto the sofa and plunks down beside me. Sticks his booted feet up on the coffee table and slings a muscled arm around me. "You're too skinny, babe. Why'd you go and lose so much weight?"

I don't answer. I just sit very still, waiting to see what he'll do. But it's impossible not to notice his smell. Sweat and sex. Was he with his new girl before he showed up here?

I rub my arm where he twisted it. My heart is beating like mad, and I feel sick with fear. I hate that he still has power over me.

"Why are you here?" I try to sound casual. Like he drops in all the time. Like we have a nice, friendly relationship.

"To see my kid."

"She doesn't want to see you." Violet is on her playmat, cooing at her reflection in the little mirror. She looks adorable. I just changed her into a clean onesie. It's white, with leaves and ladybugs.

Razor smiles down at her. He tightens his hold on my shoulder. "Sure she does. Time we got to know each other."

"Not a chance."

"Hey now, don't be so harsh. I've been thinking a guy could change for his kid."

"Don't bother. It won't change my mind."

"Bet some child support would help. I should be paying you, right?"

"I don't want your money. I don't want anything from you."

He laughs. "'Course you want money."

I pull away from him and go into the kitchen. "Want a beer?" I open the fridge, so it sounds like I'm getting him one. Then I pick my phone up from the counter.

But Razor is beside me in a second. "Don't even think about calling your brother," he says. "Or the cops." He grabs my phone, chucks it onto the counter and turns me to face him. He pulls me close, his hands on my ass. "I miss you, Jem."

I can feel him against me. I remember how my body used to respond. But not now. "Well, I don't miss you."

"My new girl, Sierra, she's just not as easygoing as you were, you know?"

"Don't know, don't care."

"She was pretty pissed off when she found out I already have a kid."

Now I care. "You *told* her?"

"It's big news. I'm a dad!"

"Does she know about the shooting too?"

He tangles the fingers of one hand in my hair. "'Course not. She knows all about you though." His other hand slides over my right butt cheek, caressing and squeezing. "Where you work, where you live." Then he whispers in my ear, "She's insanely jealous. It's her you should be scared of, not me. Oh, and the guy that did the shooting."

I don't react. I'm not taking the bait. Even though I'm scared to death of both Razor and the shooter.

He loosens his hold on me, opens a drawer and pulls out a knife. Not a big butcher knife. Just a little paring knife. But it's super sharp. He scratches the countertop with the blade. "Nice," he says. "Knife like that could do some serious damage."

Don't I know it. My heart pounds. I have to be careful not to set him off. "Okay, let's talk. What will it take?"

"For what?"

"For you not to tell the shooter who I am. And to get rid of you."

Razor tosses the knife in the sink. "Let me see my kid."

"No," I say. "Not possible." I am not making a deal with Razor. Not letting him build a relationship with Violet.

"Really?" Razor says. "Because you know it's your only chance."

I think about that for a minute. No, I can't do it. There has to be another way.

But what? I think some more, my eyes on the knife in the sink. How has it come to this? I've tried so hard to be a good mom to Violet. How can I let Razor spend time with her?

"I'm waiting," he says. "You know I can protect you. And her. I can protect you both."

"But…" I say.

"But what?"

But nothing. He's right. He is my only hope for safety.

It's a bad idea that just might work.

I have to go for it. "Fine," I say. "Here's how it will be. You can see her for one hour once a month. In a public place, like a café or park. With me present. In return, you promise not to contact us at any other time or demand any more rights. And you agree not to tell the shooter who I am or anything about me."

"Once a week."

"Once every two weeks." I don't know why I'm arguing. Razor always gets what he wants.

I'm stunned when he tilts his head and says, "Okay, I can live with that, if you swear not to rat on me."

"Deal," I say. "But how do I know I can trust you?"

"Same way I know I can trust you." He smiles down at Violet on her playmat. "For our kid's sake."

"Right," I say. "We trust each other for her."

"So we both swear on our kid," Razor says, "that we'll stick to the deal."

It feels weird and sleazy, but we both swear on Violet to keep our word.

As he leaves, Razor adds, "Hey, don't look so pissed. We're in this together now."

Chapter Twelve

God, what have I done? Made an impossible deal with Razor, that's what.

As I lock the door behind him, I have the sick feeling this won't end well. I don't want to be in this "together." Don't want him seeing Violet on a regular basis. Don't want him anywhere near us.

I pick up Violet and hug her hard. "Sorry, best little girl in the world,"

I tell her. "But your dad really wants to see you, and he's not the nicest guy." Will she someday thank me or hate me for this? "It's complicated. If the guy who shot Kwame finds me, you won't have a mom. So it's better this way."

Violet cuddles up, tucking her head between my neck and shoulder. I think about Kwame's parents and know that even though I'm in big trouble, I'm lucky. I don't get a do-over, but at least my kid is alive. The Mensahs will never see Kwame again.

Still, I really wish I hadn't made that deal with Razor. But what choice did I have? I had to agree to that so he'll protect me from the shooter. If I break my word, I'm screwed.

The cops might offer witness protection, but Razor or the shooter would find and kill me first. And even if they didn't, I'd still have to testify in court.

I can just picture how that would go. Big-shot defense lawyers would grill me and expose the ugly truth about what I did with Razor and his friends. The photos and videos would be on the news and all over the Internet for the whole world to see.

And that would be the end of my credibility and any shred of self-respect.

I guess I shouldn't be surprised that thinking about all this makes me want to call my mom. I haven't talked to her in months. Not since I let her know that Violet was born.

She wanted to come help me, but I wouldn't let her. She offered me a chance to forgive and forget, but I shut her out. Couldn't admit she was right.

I wish now that I had let her come. She's never even met Violet. Her only grandchild. All I did was send her a few photos. What a bad daughter I am.

I pick up the phone and dial her number. But she doesn't answer. The sound of her recorded voice makes me cry.

I don't bother leaving a message. What would I say? *Oh hi, Mom, just calling to say that your former best little girl in the world messed up again. Just wanted you to know I'm in deep shit. And I'm so sorry, but this might be the last time you ever hear my voice.*

After I give Violet her bottle and tuck her into her crib for the night, I break down and drink some of Wade's beer. Sneak one of the cigarettes he thinks I don't know he hides in his underwear drawer.

Then I take a shower. I need to wash the smell of smoke off me. But mostly I need to scrub away Razor's touch.

As the hot water rains down, I run my hand over my right butt cheek.

There's a rough red scar there, shaped like the letter *R*.

Exactly where Razor had his hand tonight. Reminding me who is really in charge.

I go to bed and lie awake, wishing Wade would come home. I can't tell him about Razor's visit, but I'd feel safer with him here. Way safer. Because even though Razor said he'd keep his word for Violet's sake, I don't really trust him.

But my brother has probably gone for drinks with his ball team. He won't be back for hours. I'll just have to tough it out.

I can't still my mind though.

I'm tormented by memories of the time I lived with Razor. It's hard to believe I stayed with him for so long, but he isolated me from my mom and brother and kept me drunk or drugged.

He convinced me I was worthless except as his sex toy.

Then I got pregnant. It definitely wasn't planned, and I wasn't even sure if the father was Razor or one of his friends. But I wanted to have the baby, and I figured Razor would force me to have an abortion. So I had to get out.

The night I told him I was leaving for good, he tried to stop me. Locked me in, held me down and carved his initial on my butt cheek with a knife.

But later, after he passed out, I ran. Called a taxi and showed up at Wade's. Bleeding and bawling, I begged my brother for help.

Wade said I could stay with him as long as I lived by his house rules. Which wasn't easy. There were lots of days when I wanted to bail. But I stuck it out. I had a goal. A reason for making a better life.

I had hope. So much hope. And when Violet was born, I felt like I'd been reborn.

I was a mom now. And I was going to be a good one. I was never going to let Violet find out that her father was a criminal. And I wasn't going to let Razor find out about her.

But I failed. I left my baby alone. Just for a few minutes, but that's all it took. To witness a murder. And let Razor back into my life.

Even worse, now I've let him into Violet's life.

Chapter Thirteen

Wade babysits Violet while I go to work the next morning. I have to walk past Kwame's corner again. Even more flowers and notes and toys are piled up on the sidewalk. I don't know how I'm going to get through the memorial this afternoon.

I work my shift in a daze. I don't mess up like last time, but I do watch the door in case Razor appears.

He doesn't though. But I doubt he's going to leave me alone, no matter what he agreed to. Like I said, I just don't trust him.

And I don't know if I can keep my word. I so don't want him around Violet. Sure, people can change when they have a kid, but it's hard to imagine Razor going straight.

And yes, I know fathers have rights. But I don't think fathers like Razor deserve any. He's an accomplice to murder!

He and the shooter should be locked up. And the only way to make that happen is for me to go to the cops. To hell with the consequences.

Am I brave enough to do that?

I just don't know.

When I get home, Wade and I switch roles. He goes to work. I feed Violet lunch, but I can't eat anything myself. The fact that I'm even considering ratting on Razor makes me want to throw up. It's a huge risk.

But if something happened to Violet, I'd definitely want a witness to come forward. The Mensahs deserve the truth. No matter how unpleasant.

Plus, I can't keep living in fear of Razor. And what about his new girl, Sierra? I feel sorry for her. She's probably in the same situation I was. And even if she gets away, he'll always prey on other vulnerable young girls.

It's not right for him to go free.

I have to do something.

I can't keep my word or this terrible secret any longer. And the second I make that decision, I feel a weight lifting from my heart.

I'll admit that part of my motivation is revenge. But Razor deserves everything he gets. And revenge isn't the biggest part. This is the right thing to do.

I need to act immediately. Before the memorial service. Before I change my mind.

I'm still not brave enough to face the police, so I go online to find the number for Crime Stoppers. When I start to dial, though, I lose my nerve. Their website says they're anonymous, don't have call display and don't record calls. But still. I don't think I can make the actual words come out of my mouth. I hang up.

Back on the website, I notice what is called a secure online form. I click on the link and get to work. There are a lot of boxes to fill out. I don't have all the info they ask for, but I give them Razor's name, a physical description, vehicle info and details of everything I saw.

I log off, relieved to have finally done the right thing. Razor will suspect me, but he won't know for sure.

And he'll probably rat on the shooter. Cut a deal to get a shorter sentence. But at least he'll be charged.

Hopefully, he'll be behind bars until Violet's a little older. Old enough to decide for herself if she wants to see him or not.

The memorial is starting soon, so I change Violet and put her in her cutest dress. It's pink and purple, all swirls and ruffles. Then I choose a white skirt with black flowers for myself and a black T-shirt with beading around the neck.

I put Violet in her stroller and take the elevator downstairs. People are gathering in the lobby and making their way to the common room. The media is gathered outside the building again, but only one reporter and photographer are allowed inside. I keep well away from them.

The photos of Kwame and the memorabilia have been moved into the common room. There's a podium with a microphone set up in the middle. Huge flower arrangements stand all around, giving off an overpowering smell of lilies.

The Mensahs are greeting everyone at the door. I can't avoid them any longer.

Mr. Mensah, who was so together on the TV clip, looks totally destroyed. It's his wife, Amadi, who's acting strong today. She's wearing a bright orange-and-red dress with a lacy gold shawl and the necklace Betty made. She's standing tall and proud, like she owes it to Kwame to survive this.

"I'm so, so sorry," I say, shaking Mr. Mensah's hand and hugging Amadi. "Kwame was such a great kid. We really liked him a lot. Oh, and Wade sends his condolences too. He had to work today, or you know he'd be here."

Violet is holding the rattle Kwame gave her, so I add, "Kwame found that for her at Swap Day, and she just loves it. It's her favorite toy."

If only I could tell them that they might have some answers soon. But I just say again how sorry I am.

I see Betty waving madly from across the already very crowded room. She's saved me a seat on the aisle so I can park the stroller beside me. "Well, I better go sit down."

Kwame's uncle welcomes everyone and says a few words about his nephew. Then some of Kwame's friends speak, including the girl I saw putting flowers on the shrine on the street. Finally Amadi comes up to the podium.

"We thank you all for being here with us today," she begins. "And we thank you for your support and kindness at this difficult time. Your generous donations to Kwame's memorial fund are most appreciated."

She stops and stares out at the crowd. "But now I must ask you. Who knows the truth? Who knows what happened to our boy?" Her voice rises. She looks like she's on fire in her bright dress. "We beg you, please! Somebody saw something! Please, please, end our suffering! Tell us what you know!"

I'm so glad I decided to contact the police. And I desperately hope Razor's already in custody.

Kwame's uncle invites everyone to come and help themselves to the lovely spread of food and drinks. Violet has fallen asleep in her stroller. "If you watch her," I tell Betty, "I'll go get us a cup of tea."

There's a long line for the refreshments. When I finally get back to our seats with tea and a paper plate loaded with cookies, the ground goes out from under me.

Violet's stroller is empty.

Chapter Fourteen

"Betty!" I shriek. "Where's Violet?"

Betty points across the room. "Nice girl have her."

"*What*?" I drop the tea, and it spills all over the floor. "*Who*, Betty? Who has her?" I don't see anyone holding my Violet.

"Your friend Sierra."

"I don't know any Sierra."

But Razor does.

God, I'm so stupid. He never had any intention of keeping his word.

Of course he'd send his new girl. She's probably really young. No one would suspect her of being anything other than a friend of Kwame's. And she'd do whatever Razor told her to. Even abduct Violet to scare the shit out of me.

Which totally worked.

I was right not to trust him.

Betty squints and shakes her head. "But she say she your friend."

"Well, she's not!" And to think I felt sorry for Sierra! I search the room madly. No luck. Remembering the reporters waiting outside, I head for the back door.

A black SUV is pulling away as I race out. I watch, helpless, as it disappears up the side street.

And then I'm running, faster than I ever have in my life.

I could phone, but it's only four blocks to the cop shop. Faster to run. I'm totally out of breath when I get through the doors, but still I scream, "Help! Help! Help! My baby's been abducted!"

I tell them about Razor and the shooter, about the online form, about the memorial and Sierra. It all comes out in a breathless jumble.

So much for staying anonymous.

But finding Violet is way more important.

The cops issue an Amber Alert.

A female officer who introduces herself as Paige asks me to go through everything again, slowly this time. She tells me they're already looking for Razor's vehicle. I see several officers putting on bulletproof vests and heading for their squad cars.

There's no way I'm sitting around the station, waiting. "Let me go with them,"

I beg, clinging to Paige's arm. "Please, you have to let me help find my baby."

"No, you need to stay here and make a complete statement to one of our officers," she says. "That's the best thing you can do to help your baby."

"I'll do that later," I say. "Violet's going to be so scared. She'll need me!"

"No," Paige says again.

"What if they have to negotiate? They'll want me for that."

"I'm sorry."

"Are you a mom, Paige?"

She gives me a suspicious look, like she knew I'd ask that. "Yeah, I am."

"Would *you* wait at the station?"

"We're not talking about me."

"But would you?"

She gives me another look and repeats, "This isn't about me."

"But if it was," I say, "what would you do? Wait at the station? Or go help rescue your baby?"

"Okay, okay," she finally says. "But you do exactly what I tell you to."

Then I'm in the back of a cruiser. Paige and I are screeching out of the parking lot with sirens on and lights flashing.

I've never ridden in a vehicle going so fast. We head north on the expressway. Cars pull over so we can pass.

I cling to my door handle. I can't stop shaking. My heart wants to jump right out of my throat.

Is Violet crying? Is Sierra holding her tight? "Omigod," I gasp. "What if they crash? She's not in a car seat!"

Paige turns to face me. "Please," she says. "Let the professionals handle this."

"I don't even own a car seat!" Like that's what really matters now.

"It's okay," Paige says. "We're going to get your baby back." But she doesn't sound all that sure. And her expression is grim.

She faces forward again, listens to some staticky words coming over the radio, then says, "Copy that." She turns back to me with a relieved smile. "Good news! The vehicle's been spotted!"

And then we're going even faster.

In two minutes we're pulling over beside three other squad cars. They've got a black SUV surrounded on the shoulder of the road.

"Stay in the car," Paige says.

Of course I don't. I leap out and run right up to the SUV.

But Violet's not there.

Sierra and Razor aren't there either.

There's only an older couple wearing matching wildlife T-shirts. They stand by the roadside with their hands in the air, looking ready to have matching heart attacks. Not guilty of anything but driving a black SUV with a similar license plate.

Back at the squad car, Paige says, "We're going to check out Razor's place."

We speed on up the expressway. "Hurry, hurry!" I whack the back of the seat and stamp my feet on the floor as if I can make the car go faster.

Paige turns and says, "Jemma. Please calm down. We've got this."

I take some deep breaths, but it doesn't help much. I can only pray that Violet's okay. That she's at Razor's place. Because if she's not, how will we ever find her?

We exit and head east into a quiet suburb. We can't drive as fast on the residential streets, so even though it's not far, it seems to take forever to reach Razor's house.

"Here?" Paige says when we pull up out front. The grass is cut, and there are hanging baskets full of flowers on the porch. Kids are riding bikes and skateboards on the sidewalk and playing basketball next door.

"Yeah." It looks like the typical suburban home. You'd never know what really goes on inside. Bad memories threaten to overwhelm me. But I have to stay focused. "He has the whole neighborhood fooled."

Paige shrugs and says, "Things aren't always what they seem. You stay here."

I try to open my door, but this time she's locked me in.

Chapter Fifteen

I bang on the window, but Paige doesn't look back.

Shit, shit, shit, shit, shit!

Several more police vehicles pull up. Cops in swat gear spill out and surround the house. Point their guns at the door and every window.

One of them uses a megaphone to call out a warning.

I kick at the squad-car door. Bang on the window. "Let me out! Please! Let me out!"

Nobody pays any attention. They can't even hear me. The windows are all closed up tight.

I'm going to explode with fury. Or faint from heat. I'm soaked with sweat, and there's not enough air.

Hope they don't forget I'm in here.

Then I see Razor stride out of the house. With Violet in his arms. And a knife to her back.

"Hey!" I yell, waving madly. "Bring her here!"

He wouldn't cut his own baby, would he? But it's Razor. He'd do anything!

Violet looks okay though. She's still so trusting of strangers that she's not fussing about someone she doesn't know holding her. It's a relief to see she's got Kwame's rattle in her hand.

And that she doesn't seem aware of the knife.

The cop with the megaphone puts his gun down. He walks slowly forward, with his empty hands raised in plain sight.

Razor marches down the steps. Says something to the cop. The cop confers with Paige.

Paige shakes her head. They talk some more. Then she shrugs and runs back to the squad car.

"I don't agree with this," she says as she frees me. "But he says he'll only talk to you."

I gulp for air and follow Paige. In the next few minutes, everything could work out. Or go totally wrong.

"Hey, Razor," I say. I make myself sound meek and submissive, the way he likes. I don't speak to Violet or look directly at her. I'm scared that eye contact or the sound of my voice might make her reach for me. And that then, if I don't take her, she'll start to fuss. I need her to stay still and keep playing with her rattle. "Thanks for bringing her out."

"Yeah? Well, thanks for ratting me out," he says. "Bitch. Can't believe you did that. We had a deal. You swore on our kid."

"Wait. What? You're the one who broke the deal. You promised you'd leave us alone, but you sent your girl-friend to steal my baby."

"Fuckin' hell I did," he says. "Sierra acted on her own. She just showed up here with the kid! I told you she's insanely jealous. She wanted to make trouble for me to prove her point."

Really? Should I believe him? It doesn't matter now. "That's okay," I say. "I won't press charges. Just please give me my baby back."

Violet shakes her rattle and smiles at it. Sticks it in her mouth.

"Put the knife down," the cop with the megaphone says.

Razor doesn't.

"Please," I beg him. "Please don't hurt her."

"Don't want to," he says. "But see, now we got a situation. You brought the cops here."

"Put the knife down," the cop repeats. "Now."

"Take me instead," I say to Razor. "I'll move back in and do whatever you want, but please, please, please, just let her go."

Razor smirks. "Nice try." He moves the knife closer to Violet's neck and says to the cop, "I wanna negotiate first. What do I get for cooperating?"

Violet drops her rattle. She squirms in Razor's arms and sees the knife. She smiles and reaches for it like it's a toy.

Razor swears and drops the knife.

There's an instant of stunned silence.

Then Violet starts to kick and howl.

I quickly grab her as the cops move in to take Razor down.

"Hey, hey, best little girl in the world," I comfort her as I burst into tears. "It's okay, it's okay. Mama's here now."

I can hardly hold her, I'm crying so hard. But Violet clings on like she's just figured out the danger she was in.

As the cops lead Razor to a squad car, he yells, "I didn't break our deal, Jem. And I still want visiting rights. I want to know my kid."

I can't even. I have no words. I just sob and clutch Violet to me like I'll never let her go.

"You okay?" Paige asks.

I watch as the squad car takes Razor away. "I am now."

Chapter Sixteen

Paige picks up the rattle and holds the mirror so Violet can peek into it. Violet giggles at her reflection. And then I'm telling Paige about Kwame, and how he gave the rattle to Violet.

"Wow. That's so sad," she says.

"Yeah. Sometimes life really sucks."

"I know," she says. "Man, do I know.

But you and your beautiful baby are safe now. You can move on."

"I guess." I stroke Violet's hair and kiss her cheeks and tell her, "Oh, you are the best little girl in the world." Then I turn to Paige. "I don't want to go to court though. I can't testify against Razor."

"Don't worry," she says. "It probably won't come to that. His lawyer will cut a deal to avoid a trial. But he and the shooter will both go away for a long time." She steers me to a squad car. "You should go home and relax. Is there someone you can call?"

"Yeah, my brother."

I text Wade on the way back to the station, and he's there waiting for us. Apparently, he kicked everybody out of the Bean Leaf and put up the Closed sign.

He doesn't give me hell. We both know there'll be lots of time for explanations, so he doesn't even ask any questions. He just holds me and Violet tight.

When I'm finished giving my full statement to the cops, Wade says, "Let's go home."

Since we live so close by, we don't need a ride. And we don't want to be dropped off at Woodley Co-op in a police car anyway. Don't want the media or nosy residents to see that.

Wade didn't think to retrieve the stroller from the common room, so I carry Violet in my arms. She snuggles close to me, making those sweet *mmmmm* sounds I'm sure mean "mama." My mind races as we walk, trying to process everything that's happened.

But that's going to take a while. Even locked up, Razor will haunt me for a long time yet. Probably forever. Because apart from anything that happened between us, he's still Violet's dad. I have to accept and deal with that.

Should I believe him about Sierra acting on her own? I'd like to, for

Violet's sake. Then someday, when I have to explain things to her, I'll be able to say he kept his word. He honored our deal because he wanted to have contact with her. And when she reached for the knife, he dropped it so she wouldn't get hurt.

We'll see how it goes.

But Paige is right. For now we're safe, and that's all that matters.

As we cross the park in front of our building, I remember the party last Saturday night. The night I foolishly left Violet alone and went to the store. Seems like weeks or months ago, not just four days.

"I'm so sorry," I tell Wade. "I'll explain everything when we get home. I mean, if you don't have to go back to work."

"It's okay," he says. "If I can't find somebody to cover for me, we'll just stay closed."

"You're not going to like what you hear."

"Figured that out already." He stops short and points to a TV crew camped outside the front of our building. "Great. They're still here." We turn and go around to the back.

I'm not sure if the reporters are waiting for the Mensahs or me or all of us. But I know it's only a matter of time before my past with Razor hits the news. And the Internet.

Still, as long as Violet's here with me, who really cares? Some things can never be undone. We just have to find a way to live with the messy consequences. In my head I practice saying, *No comment. Please respect our privacy. No comment.*

We take the stairs because we don't want to meet anybody in the elevator. Wade offers to carry Violet up, but I'm

not letting go. I hug her close to my heart.

Wade unlocks our apartment and opens the door for us. "Christ, it's hot in here. We gotta get that air conditioner fixed."

"Yeah, really," I say as he pours us some cold drinks and makes up Violet's bottle. Then we sit together on the sofa while I feed her.

I start at the beginning. It takes a while. It's hard to talk about what I witnessed and even harder to admit what I did. But I give him all the details.

"Forgive me?" I ask when I'm done.

Wade shrugs and gets up to start dinner. He doesn't speak for a long time. But finally he says, "I'm just glad you're both okay. And you'll never do something so stupid again, right?" His parental tone is so comforting.

"Right," I say. "Promise."

We eat leftover chicken and salad. When we're done, he says, "Can you look into getting the air conditioner fixed?"

"Sure. First thing tomorrow." I happen to know that Dekker has a list of repair places in the office. Not that I'm looking for an excuse to go see him or anything. But maybe we can set up a time for that coffee. And if he wants to listen, I have a lot to tell him.

I'll visit Betty and the Mensahs soon too. Might even try calling my mom again. But for now, I'm just happy to be home with my brother and my baby.

ACKNOWLEDGMENTS

With deepest thanks to my family and everyone at Orca.

Jocelyn Shipley is the author of several books for young adults, including *Shatterproof* in the Orca Currents series. Her award-winning stories have been published in newspapers and anthologies, and her work has been translated into many languages. Born and raised in London, Ontario, Jocelyn now splits her time between Toronto and Vancouver Island. For more information, visit www.jocelynshipley.com.